FOR VIV AND GIGI

Carolrhoda Books
A division of Lerner Publishing Group, Inc.
241 First Avenue North
Minneapolis, MN 55401 USA

For reading levels and more information, look up this title at www.lernerbooks.com.

Designed by Lindsey Owens.
Main body text set in Avenir LT Pro 21/24.
Typeface provided by Linotype AG.
The illustrations in this book were created with pencil, printmaking paper, watercolor, Corel Painter, and a Wacom tablet.

Library of Congress Cataloging-in-Publication Data

Names: Kulka, Joe, author, illustrator.
Title: Undercover ostrich / by Joe Kulka.
Description: Minneapolis : Carolrhoda Books, [2019] | Summary: "A curious narrator tries to figure out why sneaky ostriches go undercover" —Provided by publisher.
Identifiers: LCCN 2018004551 (print) | LCCN 2018010524 (ebook) | ISBN 9781541541825 (eb pdf) | ISBN 9781512497878 (lb : alk. paper)
Subjects: | CYAC: Ostriches—Fiction. | Undercover operations—Fiction. | Humorous stories.
Classification: LCC PZ7.K9490153 (ebook) | LCC PZ7.K9490153 Und 2019 (print) | DDC [E]—dc23

LC record available at https://lccn.loc.gov/2018004551

Manufactured in the United States of America
1-43514-33313-6/5/2018

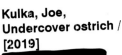
UNDERCOVER OSTRICH

JOE KULKA

 CAROLRHODA BOOKS • MINNEAPOLIS

I NOTICE THINGS.

For example, I notice a lot of animals are super sneaky.

A chameleon can change colors to stay hidden.

Where did he go?

Possums can pretend to be dead—even when they are not!

TOO TRICKY!

But do you know who
is the sneakiest of all?

UNDERCOVER OSTRICHES!

They are everywhere.

I've been keeping an eye on them.

They are experts at blending into their surroundings.

Can you see the ostrich?
It is difficult because he is undercover.

I'll give you a hint.
He's in one of the birdbaths.

I KNOW! Hard to find, right?

It took me several hours to realize this was *not* a picture of two woodpeckers.

Those ostriches must
be up to something!

Undercover ostriches can go undetected in broad daylight . . .

or in pale moonlight.

Undercover ostriches can sneak
by unseen in the country . . .

and even in the city!

An ostrich could be in your house right now, and you would never know it.

You might even mistake the ostrich for one of your pets.

Mostly they hang out
in the backyard . . .

But *what* is that tricky ostrich trying to do?!

AHA! So this is why they go undercover!

To steal food from the squirrels!

AN UNDERCOVER ELEPHANT.